JEAN DE BRUNHOFF

BABAR
AND HIS CHILDREN

Translated from the French
by Merle Haas.

Random House · New York.
1989

Other books by Jean de Brunhoff
in this series

The Story of Babar
The Travels of Babar
Babar the King
Babar and Father Christmas

One morning Babar said to Cornelius:
"Old friend, you who have been my constant companion
through good times and bad,
listen now to my wonderful news.
Celeste, my wife,
has just told me that she is expecting
a baby."
Then, pointing to the footstool, he continued:
"Here is a new hat for you
and also a message
I have just written
to my subjects.
Take it and read it aloud
to all the inhabitants of Celesteville."

After having congratulated and thanked Babar,
Cornelius puts on his full-dress uniform.
Standing before the gateway of the Royal Palace,
he tells his drummer to assemble the townspeople.

Slowly he unfurls the King's proclamation,
puts on his spectacles, and reads in a loud voice.
The elephants, gathered together in large numbers,
listen respectfully.

B

Dear and Loyal Subjects

When you hear a salute fired
from a cannon, do not be
alarmed. It will not mean
that another war has begun,
but simply that a little baby
has been born to your King
and Queen in the Royal Palace.
    In this way you will all
learn the glorious tidings at
the same time.

Long live the future Mother,
your Queen Celeste!

Babar

Here, reproduced exactly,
is Babar's message, which Cornelius read.

Babar is trying to read
but finds it difficult to concentrate;
his thoughts are elsewhere. He tries to write,
but again his thoughts wander.
He is thinking of his wife
and the little baby soon to be born.
Will it be handsome and strong?
Oh, how hard it is to wait
for one's heart's desire!

Celeste urges him to go for a ride on his bicycle,
to take his mind off the big event,
and Babar finally consents.
After having pedaled several miles,
he finds a pleasant spot and decides to rest.
Seated on the grass, he admires the surrounding countryside,
Celesteville and Fort Saint John. "It is from there
that the cannon will be fired," he says to himself.

At this very moment:
Boom!
Babar hears the salute.
"There it goes! What a shame that I wasn't at home!"
thinks Babar.
He immediately mounts his bicycle
and rides home
as fast as he can pedal.

There, up on the turret,
the Artillery Captain of the King's Guard
carries out the orders he has just received
by telephone.
He gives the command.
One blank shot is fired,
then another, and finally
a third.

The elephants gather in groups on the promenade
and begin to wonder and ask questions.
King Babar had only mentioned
one shot.
Why did the gunners fire off three?
Cornelius himself cannot understand it.

Babar reaches home
quite breathless from his fast ride.
He also had heard three shots.
He dashes headlong up the stairs,
joyfully rushes into Celeste's bedchamber,
and embraces his wife
tenderly.

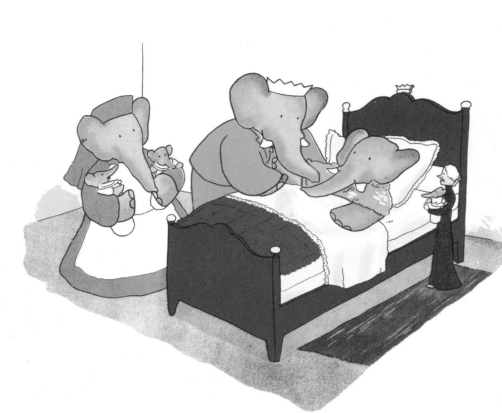

She smiles and proudly
shows him three little
baby elephants.
That explains everything.
One salute
for each child;
three babies = three salutes.
But what a surprise
to find three babies
when you only
expected one!

The Old Lady has one in her arms, and the
nurse holds the other two. Arthur and Zephir are
terribly excited. Babar has given them permission
to come and see the babies. They walk in quietly.
"Oh! How tiny!" says Zephir. "Oh! How cute!" adds
Arthur, as he admires the baby lying in the cradle.

Celeste had prepared
only one cradle;
so the nurse quickly
makes another one
out of a wash basket,
a towel, and
an umbrella.
It is crude,
but the babies
are warm
and sheltered.

Here are the babies, settled now in the garden
and asleep in a big perambulator.
Babar and Celeste receive the congratulations of their friends.
Almost everyone brings a gift.

Poutifour, the farmer, and his wife bring fruits from their own orchard; the hens offer some eggs; the gardener some flowers. The bakers present a huge cake, and Cornelius brings three silver rattles.

Now Babar and Celeste have to find three names
for their children. Of course
they had discussed this beforehand.
Pom, Pat, or Peter? Julius, John, or Jim?
Alexander? Emil? Baptiste?
Alexander isn't bad,
but what if it's a girl?
Juliet, Virginia, or...
"We'll simply have to come to a decision
about their names," says Celeste to Babar.
"I'd like our daughter to be named Flora."
"I'd like that too," says Babar,
"and as for the two boys, I think
we might choose Pom and Alexander."
After having repeated Pom, Flora, and Alexander
in one voice, Babar and Celeste declare:
"That's perfect. Let's keep these names."

Every week Dr. Capoulosse puts the babies
in his big scale and weighs them.
One day he says to Celeste : "Your Majesty,
the babies aren't gaining fast enough anymore.
You must supplement their feeding
with six bottles of cows' milk,
to which you must add a tablespoonful of honey."
The little ones soon get used to the bottles.
Arthur and Zephir like
to watch them drink.
Pom is the greediest
and the fattest.
He is the one
on Celeste's lap.
He always cries
when his bottle is empty.

1

Flora is very good
and lies in her cradle
playing with the rattle
which Cornelius gave her.

2

She throws it up in the air
with her trunk.
What a nice jingly noise
it makes!

3

She puts it
in her mouth
and sucks it.
What fun!

4

Suddenly,
she doesn't
quite know how,
she swallows it.

She chokes,
gets purple in the face,
and her trunk trembles.
Celeste rushes to her.

She grabs her, turns her
upside down, and shakes
her. But still the rattle
won't fall out.

Fortunately
Zephir manages
to pull it out
with his hand.

Flora is saved, but she
cries most bitterly.
Her mother tries
to comfort her.

Now the children begin to run about and play
in their big sunny nursery.
Babar often comes in to play with them.
Today, he sits Pom on the end of his trunk
and bounces him up and down.
It's like our game "Ride a Cock Horse."

Cornelius hangs the ropes of a swing
from the end of each tusk,
and Arthur gently rocks Alexander back and forth.
The boys have learned to walk before their sister.
Flora will soon follow their example.
She can stand up alone already.

When the children are dressed,
the nurse takes them out for a ride
in their big carriage.
They are still too young to walk very far.
One day Nurse says to Arthur:
"It is colder than I thought
and we are not far from the house.
It won't take me long to run back and
get some sweaters so my babies won't catch cold.
Will you look after them for me until I come back?"
Arthur is very glad to be trusted and proudly pushes the carriage.

He pushes it twenty feet forward, then twenty feet back,
and takes good care to avoid the stones.
All of a sudden he hears the soldiers parading.
As he turns around to watch them,
he lets go of the pram.
The path is slightly downgrade at this point,
and the carriage begins to roll off by itself.
Pom, Flora, and Alexander
think this is very funny and laugh,
but Arthur is frightened and runs after them.
The grade gets steeper and steeper.

The carriage rolls faster and faster.
Now the children are scared too.
Arthur runs after it as fast as he can.
Nurse comes back with the sweaters.
Very much worried, she joins the chase.
It looks as though the babies were in grave danger.
Just a bit farther on there is a bend in the road
with a deep ravine on one side.
The carriage must be stopped before the bend
or it will go straight on down into the ravine, and then...
The accident!
Martha, the turtle,
out for a stroll,
has seen it all coming
and understands the situation thoroughly.

She hurries along on her short legs.
Just as the carriage is about
to topple over the precipice,
she succeeds in throwing herself under the wheels!
Suddenly checked while going full tilt,
the carriage stops and almost turns over.
Pom and Flora are jolted back
against the hood, which saves them,
but poor Alexander
is thrown out head first. Nurse screams
and the rabbit runs away.

Mr. and Mrs. Squirrel have heard the nurse's scream. Then, a minute later they hear the rustle of leaves and the noise of breaking branches to the left above them. They both look up and see the head of a baby elephant. He is yelling for his mother in a frightened lisp. "Mama! Alessander's falling! Mama! Help Alessander!"

"Steady, little elephant!
Don't let go!
We're coming!"
cry the squirrels.
"Just balance yourself
and try to get your foot
up on that big branch.
We're right here.
Don't be afraid.
We'll help you!"

Their scheme succeeds.
Mr. Squirrel gives further orders.
"Hold fast to my tail
and wiggle your big ears
to keep your balance!
Watch your step!
Follow me!
You can rest when
you've reached our shelter!"
A few minutes later,
safe and sound
in the squirrels' hole,

Alexander breathes a sigh of relief.
How lucky he was
to have fallen in the trees,
and to have found these obliging friends!
He might have been badly hurt!
Now he'd like to go
and tell his Mama not to worry.
But how can he get down
that tree trunk?
It is absolutely smooth and very high!
Just then a big giraffe strolls by
and sees his plight. He says:
"Look here, little elephant,
I'll put my head right close to the branch.

Then you can sit down between my ears
and hold on to my horns.
I know your parents
and I'll take you back to them".
Alexander, quite delighted, says good-bye
to the squirrels and thanks them.
He settles himself on the giraffe's head
and off they go.
Although the giraffe walks slowly,
Alexander decides that he prefers his perambulator.
Informed by the nurse, Babar and Celeste
are already on their way to the scene of the accident.
What joy to be reunited!
Arthur is ever so pleased.

A few months later,
Babar decides it would be fun to go on a picnic.
The weather is fine, and the family is in high spirits.
Cornelius feels the heat but joins them enthusiastically.
Later, tired and hungry, they all sit down
to a delicious lunch.

After the meal Celeste tidies things up.
Babar goes off to fish in a nearby stream.
Cornelius lies down in the shade to have a nap.
Alexander mischievously wriggles under Cornelius' derby hat
and walks about with short steps.
"That's a funny - looking tortoise!" says Pom.

While playing, they come to the edge of the river.
Alexander has another bright idea.
He puts the hat in the water. "Nice boat!" says he,
as he steps in to try it. "It floats! Isn't that marvelous?"

Just then the current catches the hat,
and it drifts away from the bank.
Alexander is enchanted with his boat ride,
but Pom and Flora are a bit worried.

How can they get the hat
back to shore?
Flora begins to cry.
She runs off
to call her Mama,
who was just beginning
to wonder where
the children could be.
Pom runs along
the bank calling:
"Alexander, come back!
Please, nice little ducks,
oh, please bring my brother back!"
But the ducks fly away.
Suddenly, Pom
gives a lusty yell:
"A crocodile! A crocodile!"

Alexander looks around. "Oh! Papa!" he whimpers.
Babar was peacefully fishing
and thought the children were playing.
As he hears this desperate cry for help,
he understands that something serious must have happened.
He stands up and trumpets angrily
as he sees the horrible crocodile.

Three seconds in which to act - and no gun!
The situation seems hopeless!
Babar, without hesitating a moment, grabs the anchor
and hurls it violently into the monster's jaws.
Caught like a fish, the crocodile, in a wild fit of rage,
flips his tail right out of the water.
Tossed about by the swirling eddy,
the hat capsizes and Alexander is thrown into the river.

Babar dives in after him and searches about with his trunk.
Ah! He feels something!
Hurrah! It's Alexander's ear!
He makes quick work of bringing him up out of the water
and reviving him.
As to the crocodile, he thrashes madly about
but cannot rid himself of either
the anchor
or the boat.

The birds gather around Babar and Alexander,
who are of course dripping wet.
"Would you be kind enough," asks Babar,
"to go and reassure Queen Celeste?
Ask her to hurry back to the house to lay out some dry clothes
and prepare hot drinks for us.
And you, dear little ducklings," he adds,
"would you be kind enough to dive down
and bring back my crown and Cornelius' hat?
They are down at the bottom of the river."

Alexander kisses his Mama happily.
She bathes him, gives him a good rubdown,
and puts him to bed under heavy blankets.
Arthur, Zephir, Pom, and Flora
are still very excited.
The big flamingo brings back
the crown and the hat.
"Oh, thank you very much," says Babar.
"The hat is slightly damp
and out of shape.
Cornelius, however, will be happy to have it back
because it is an old keepsake."

Now everyone is asleep.
Babar and Celeste will soon go to bed too.
They are gradually calming down
after all these exciting events.
"Truly it is not easy
to bring up a family,"
sighs Babar.
"But how nice the babies are!
I wouldn't know how to get along
without them anymore."